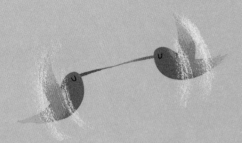

For Zoë – I really, really
love you, Zo!
~ K. N.

For Ffion & Iolo
~ D. B.

tiger tales
5 River Road, Suite 128, Wilton, CT 06897
Published in the United States 2023
Originally published in Great Britain 2023
by Little Tiger Press Ltd.
Text copyright © 2023 Karl Newson
Illustrations copyright © 2023 Duncan Beedie
ISBN-13: 978-1-6643-0018-7
ISBN-10: 1-6643-0018-X
Printed in China
LTP/2800/4805/0622

www.tigertalesbooks.com

I REALLY, REALLY LOVE YOU SO

by
KARL NEWSON

Illustrated by
DUNCAN BEEDIE

tiger tales

I really, really, really, really,
REALLY LOVE YOU SO!

I thought that I should tell you,
just in case you didn't know . . . .

There is nothing better than a **great big hug** with you!

I really, really **love** you so.

I do.   I do.

I
DO!

I'd like to find a special way
to show the **love in me** . . . .
I'll wrestle with a crocodile!

I'll sail right out to **sea!**

No....

. . . I'll climb the **tallest** mountain,

and I'll write it in the

snow!

It's really, really, really, **REALLY COLD** UP HERE, you know!

Maybe you'd prefer a bunch of **flowers?**

Or a stick?

Maybe I could find a **hat** and do a **magic** trick!

Maybe
I could **make you**
something
special,
like a card . . .

or a robot . . .

or a r o c k e t.

WHY

IS

MAKING

THINGS

SO HARD??

A-ha!

I'll watch the **other animals**
and **copy** what they do!

I stompy-**STOMPY**,
tooty-tooty,
really love you so!

I chirpy-chirpy,
squawky-
squawky,
really do,
you
know!

I love you from **the bottom** to the **top** of every tree!

I love you

when I'm running

while a **bear** is

chasing me!

I love you when I'm hiding, and I love you when—

"They went that way! They're not here!"

OH, DEAR!

It's time for
a disguise . . . .

I love you when you're snoring like a lion (and you do)....

Love is like a
sparkle
and a **twinkle**
in my toes . . . .

It **tingles** in my **tummy** . . .

and it tickles in
my nose!

And I thought that I should tell you,
just in case you didn't know . ...

. . . I really, really,
really, **really,**
REALLY
LOVE
YOU SO!